DEDICATION

"To my earthbound children, Damiano, Nina, Destiny and
Johnathan, I DID IT! Thank you for believing in me and
encouraging me to be great. To my daughter Nina, thank you
for coming in clutch with the title of this book. I love yous more
than tongue can tell, and more than time can measure.

"She was different. She didn't have money, or worldly possessions.

What she had was most valuable. She had a free spirit. She was a healer. For that reason, she was hunted. Hunted by men who only wanted to steal her healing powers. They would never truly care for her. They would never truly love her, forcing her to hide, scared to feel, scared to love, and scared to be seen"

Life Lessons

With a life full of purpose,
I wonder when it will end
I'm not scared to meet my maker,
Over the years he's been a friend.
I have learned so much this lifetime,
I had to grab my pen.
I have learned to be forgiving
It's really for ourselves
We must deal with real emotions
Instead, of leaving them on shaky shelves
I have learned to love
And to love with real intentions
I have learned to move on from things,
and not to always attack with vengeance.
I have learned that when one door closes
A better one will open
I have learned to tell people you love them
Instead of leaving with words unspoken
I have learned that when a stranger loves you
Don't take that shit for granted
It's from these relationships that grow
from loving seeds that have been planted
I have learned that when you love someone
Always do it unconditionally,
only then, will you know a soul so free

Toxic Love

Trying to let go of a love so rare.
The kind of love you can't even compare,
To anything even worldly bound
This toxic love though, is truly profound.
since the very beginning, since we both locked
eyes your spirit, your soul,
spoke to mine, no lies!
Over these years,
We've seen each other grow.
Through trials and tribulations
 No matter what, we always go with the flow.
 Now things have changed and I'm needing you.
 You have a family, how am I selfish? I have one too.
Remember ME?
I've BEEN deeply in love with you.
but things have changed,
now I'm trying to hold on also realizing,
how our souls are drawn
at the same time if I leave,
I'll be plagued with thoughts of you every eve.
I'm in an emotionally, soulful,
compromised, hostage situation.
my unconditional love, loyalty, and respect for you
has no motherfucking expiration.
I've been trying to get you to understand,
This toxic love was never my intention,
 this shit was never planned.
 however, this union, this love,
 this "thing" we share for one another,
 Is the reason why we could never
 Truly give our "all" to any other.

Time Goes on...

As I turn the pages on pictures from long ago
I can't help but look into the eyes of those around me
If you look close enough, deep enough
Their eyes can tell a story
Looking back on childhood memories
Family was all around
Block parties, outings to the park
All the major holidays
Remembering in real time
How I wanted to feel loved like this always
The feeling of security and family
Not knowing that there was a storm brewing
Slowly creeping, eventually manifesting
Into a Demon the size of New York City
The family I once held near
Held dear to my heart
Was violently, aggressively being torn apart
No goodbyes, no hugs
No see you later gator
No warm smiles, no familiar faces
No more fun exiting places
These pictures, they hold a secret indeed
While yes, we smiled it looked so effortlessly
But deeper behind their eyes
Nobody really cared, loved
Or even fucked with me
I'm a product of two selfish people
Who pretended to care
Who looked me in my eyes
And said they would ALWAYS be there...

Soul Cry

Whenever you're near me
My heart starts to sing.
I trust your touch,
This isn't just a fling.
When our bodies collide
It's like a perfect fit.
I could never again imagine us in a split.
I not only want you; I need you too.
Do you even know how long
I've been in love with you?
This love for you started so very long ago.
Maybe we were lovers?
Maybe even a foe?
Whatever it was,
our souls are aware,
Of the crazy amount of love
that we share.
Because how in this lifetime,
We can't get enough.
We always crave each other's kisses.
We always crave each other's touch.
When we're not together,

my soul starts to cry.
I can't think of life anymore.
All my soul wants to do is die.
but when the time comes,
to see your face
My soul is ready,
for our magical embrace

FED UP

I'm tired of always feeling like this.
I'm exhausted of trying,
To get you to see I exist.
I take care of you, emotionally.
I love you mentally.
But all you manage to do,
Is suck the fucking life
Right out of me
Whenever you're sick
My healing hands provide protection.
When you're feeling down
My sexiness provides you with an erection.
I've been sick with a fever.
I've even been sleep.
You, never caring about,
Love or intimacy.
Only interested in
Making me feel cheap.
I'm tired of all this,
back and forth we go.
I'm tired of you treating me,
Like your little whore.
You want to entertain,
and talk to other females.
Your stupid ass only speaks
of lies and tall tales.
I'm sick of it, I'm tired.
I'm done, done, no longer dumb, dumb!
I'm no longer allowing you,
To treat me like scum.
I'm worthy, I'm dope!
You wasted my time.
I've finally come to terms,
you will never be mine

9110024: revised

It's been a long time,
Since I felt this way.
In my head, you have to go.
In my heart, I want you to stay.
With every touch,
My heart beats faster and faster.
I need to please you,
You are my master.
The way you kissed me,
The expression in your eyes.
I want to tell you I love you,
But you'll think I'm telling lies.
You didn't listen to my demands,
Of, "harder!"
You took care of my body,
Not your ego, that's smarter.
I could feel your excitement,
Rushing through me.
I see myself with you
Happy and carefree
What the hell is going on?
I can't help this feeling,
That we belong.
I'm not sure if it's true love yet.
My heart is open, so we're all set
I want to be more than just friends.
Could we? Or this fling has come to an end?
Before you go, I need you to know,
You're the first person to touch me,
And make me feel whole!

Twin Flame kind of Love

You come to me in my dreams,
telling me you love me.
How I make you feel, your soul is free
For those few seconds that no words are spoken,
Your eyes are screaming for me to help you,
You can't speak, you're choking
Your mouth is moving, but I can't hear
Your eyes though are mine, I am a seer
I see what your eyes see.
I can hear what your mouth won't speak
Don't you know, I'm the only one who
can see and feel your genuine mystique?
Once you stop fighting, what keeps us bonded
You'll soon find out, why our love was founded
We keeping trying to find, what we feel is missing
It's only then, when we start kissing,
Our SOULS only NEED and CRAVE each other
This is why, it will never truly work with another

"He said that he's in love with me. I'm not in love with him. He wants to carry me away in his ocean of love. Unfortunately for him, I cannot swim. He wants to watch the sunset in my deep brown eyes. When he's near me, my body feels safe, but all my ears hear are lies."

Transformation

You tell me not to compare you,

to the men that broke my heart.

They all said they loved me,

Until death do us part.

But your lies turned into venom,

like a sword stabbing my heart.

One had a problem with women,

fucking around and round we go,

the other addicted to Yayo.

They would also put their hands on me,

like a ritual that sacrificed animals.

One would chew me up, not spitting me out,

like a bunch of fucking cannibals.

I cooked; I had a clean house.

I would even fuck them,

while my bloody nose ran down my face,

onto my fucking blouse.

I've sacrificed myself, mind, body, and soul.

Loving them while they hated me.

After dealing with them

I would never truly be whole.

let's not even talk about the kids.

I thought if I stayed,

the kids would be better than me.

I didn't want them to be fuck ups God forbid.

You promised you wouldn't hurt me like them!

That's exactly what the fuck you did!

You knew all these niggas hurt me.

Broke me right down to my core.

Here you go again talking to bitches,

Once again, my heart tore.

I'm supposed to forgive and forget,

is what you said to me.

Then you continued to hurt me

hitting the point of no return with no regret!

I can do all these things, right back to you.

that's what you've done to me for years.

This time it's going to be you that's crying,

And no one to wipe away your fucking tears!

You do nothing to be consistent.

I'm always taking your little crumbs.

So, forgive me if I'm always sad.

And why I'm always so fucking numb.

You were the one that was to keep me good.

Instead, it was you who betrayed me.

I tried; I did all I could.

I can't stay here much longer,

Or I will surely die.

Depression Strikes

So much is going on in my head.
Wanting and wishing that I was dead.
Hoping someone will hear my call.
On top of the building, waiting to fall.
Is this how my life,
was destined to be?
Flying, soaring in heaven free?
What will my kids think?
What would they say?
Would they want me to go?
Or wish me to stay?
How about the husband,
so handsome, so true.
Should I tell him,
he's the reason
I always feel blue?
My family hates me.
No one to help.
Everybody's always,
thinking about themselves.
What happens to me?
I'm pushed away in the back.
When I speak of wisdom
they want to attack.
So, I ask what is my purpose here?
Am I just patiently waiting,
for my end to be near?
I'm hoping someone,
will hear my call.
I'm on top of the building,
waiting to fall

Energy doesn't Lie

I find myself thinking about you.
Hearing you whisper
your admiration for me,
without moving your lips.
Your eyes soft and deep,
Forcing my soul to speak.
The way my body calls for you…
Silently yet screaming.
Softly and caringly.

Your hands coat my skin,
For an extra layer of protection.
Knowing that in your arms I am safe.
Just the thought of you,
makes my hips Sway…
back and forth, back, and forth, back and forth...

My body can't hide my affection for you.

Feeling your lips construct my shadow,
In a graceful silhouette.
How do I begin to explain
what your presence does to me?
It's been years since you've touched me…
I can still feel it as if it was hours ago.

Telling you would be against the rules.

So, I just sit here and think about you…
Perfectly, charmingly, obsessively…
Wondering if I've crossed your mind…
Silently, patiently waiting...

Until the day you're finally mine.

Introduction to 12th Anniversorry

"Hello", said the heart to the brain let's have a seat there's a lot to explain. I know when he yells it's not his fault. His mother fucked his head up, he's miserable by default."

12th Anniversorry: A Recap

This year hasn't been the best,
but I don't feel it's been the worst.
I'm sorry things happened the way they did,
sometimes I feel so cursed.
Maybe if we dance to our wedding song,
every time it came on.
We would always remember,
having, that feeling of our first day,
a month before November.
Maybe if you prioritized me as I did for you,
maybe you wouldn't have chosen your game,
maybe you wouldn't have made me feel blue.
Maybe it was all the bitches, attention,
you were so got damn eager to keep.
You been doing weird shit in my face.
I've been knowing you was a fucking creep.
The look in your eyes as I would cry.

I would beg and plead for you to stop,
with all the fucking lies.
We've lost a lot of things,
as these times have slowly passed.
We even lost each other.
I really thought we would last.
You have stripped away my self- esteem,
liking every big booty hoe out there.
If only your face lit up,
like it did with porn,
maybe we would have been a good pair.
All the lies you told.
All the love you didn't care to mold.
All the things we talked about doing.
All the disrespect.
All the faux wooing.
The way I cried when you chose other women
how my heart broke, how I felt inhuman.
You would trigger me,
leaving me abandoned
in my emotional times of need.
You would look at me, smirk, not giving a fuck,

about anything not even one plea.
Every opportunity you had,

To make me feel like shit,

you would come in on your ego driven horse.

Battering myself esteem,
shattering my idea of intercourse.

You would have your way with me anyways,
Taking what I held most dear.

You didn't care about my emotional state,
you didn't care about my fear.

I had to still be intimate with you,

regardless of what you've done.

Sometimes I wish I would have died that day,
somebody hand me a fucking gun!

I know I'm still here, but I'd rather be there.

You've implanted so much fear inside me.
I wish this life wasn't so crappy.
Speaking to other bitches
while I lay here alone and cried.
I couldn't believe you were just like him,
I wanted to fucking die!

you have never put me first,

while you were making random bitches feel good.

How many times was I embarrassed

Always triggering me,
bringing me back to my childhood.

You never made sure I was safe.

If I had to compare how I'm feeling, I feel chafed.

I can keep going but my heart can't take it anymore.

I tell you this though, this is the last time,

you knocked my ass down to the floor.

So, to wrap this up,

looking back on years of abuse

from your narcissistic hands,

Let me ask you one question?
You still think you're a fucking man?

In any case, I'm not sure,

how this anniversorry could be happy.

You ruined us, and you been fucking sloppy

Can You See Me?

Waiting and waiting for someone anyone
to see me to notice me.
To recognize my smile when I laugh.
Someone to see ME.
To see my soul, my passions, my love.
To see my life in their eyes.
I need someone to hold me,
my secrets, my dreams, my heart.
Someone that I can feel from across the room.
That feeling when your spirit starts to jump up and down,
Up and down, up and down.
With every step, closer, and closer and closer we get.
I need someone who can taste me,
my hunger and my determination.
To be loved by someone unconditionally.
To taste how sweet my love for them is.
Sweat running down my face, my lips, my neck.
The sweetness of your kisses, your touch, your lips on my back.
Where is that someone?
That someone who can smell all our achievements together?
Even before they've been accomplished
That someone who has a nose for success,
for love, for excitement?
I would tell him things,
I, myself, have longed to hear.
I love you; I miss you; I got you,
I'll always be near.
The words that my mouth has spoken,
a million times to fall upon deaf ears.
I would listen, I would hear, I would comprehend.
I will learn, I will embrace until the very end.
I have longed for the day,
that someone would see ME.

Always there for me

So many things I want to tell you.
There are many things I want to say.
Like, how I think about you,
each and every day.
How I always want to hold you.
Especially when I'm scared.
When I thought nobody loved me
You always showed you cared.
How I feel so safe when you're by my side.
This love affair, I can no longer hide.
With you my soul feels incredibly free.
I can talk how I talk, be who I am.
Let's drive into the sunset,
you're my best man.
However, when it's time to leave you,
my spirit really cries.

It cries because I need you.
Who knows when I'll see you again?
so, I started writing love letters,
I always have my pen.
You told me you didn't need me.
Or love me like back in the day?
my spirit is screaming and crying,
how I wanted you to stay.
When I look into your eyes
I knew you told me no lies.
Your situation prevented you from me.
I go to sleep thinking about you.
And what we could be.
I wake up with only you on my mind,
my hearts beating for you like a drum.
During the day you're on my mind,
but you're not here and once again and I'm alone.
My love for you is selfish and blind.
Something is bothering me, what do I do?
How the fuck could I even fall for you?

The Affair: a short

I don't really know who you are.
We've never discussed "us" thus far.
Are we both in love? How could this be?
I can't be with you, I'm married.
We would lay in bed together.
Me wanting this to last forever.
Something in your eyes.
Something that never lies.
but your actions hurt.
What was this? Just a flirt?
When our bodies would meet
It was hard to be discreet.
I just wanted your body to touch mine.
How you looked at me,
kissed me, oh, so fine.
Knowing nothing about each other's lives,
So, how could it be, I wanted to be your wife?
Confused about you, knowing how I felt.
We had a crazy hand,
that the Universe dealt.
Time passes thinking of you from time to time.
Wondering why I didn't make you mine.
I know eventually you would cause me pain,
Just loving you in my mind,
is driving me insane.

The Narcissist and His Mask

We started out talking about the stars,
up all night, it felt like a stalking.
The world was ours.
I moved in with kids,
it was new for us all.
You told me you got us,
you would never let us fall.
As time went on, the sex got weird.
I tried and tried to be sexy,
your ego was smeared.

Not knowing it could be cachexy.
I never shamed you,
but you needed a fight.
not knowing you had other women,
I still cried and cried all night.
That's why you were never there.
I'm tired and I'm always sad.

My heart is tired of this despair.

When He's Near

When I see you, I get so excited.
My walk feels different, my hair sways different.
My face is smiling, I'm just different.
When I'm with you, I feel safe.
We laugh a lot.
When you touch me,
my soul leaves my body.
We're moving to the beat of our hearts.
Slow and steady…
It speeds up with excitement,
It slows down with love.
When I'm near you, I'm happy.
My soul jumps up and down
with the overwhelming feelings,
of nostalgia, of home...
I feel like our souls
remember each other from the past…
the way past...

I'm happiest here with you.
I'm comfortable feeling your body heat
from across the room
I'm safe, I'm home. I'm in love with you.

If I died today...

If I died today
What would you think?
What would you say?
Would you say I loved my family?
Would you say my love was true?
Can you say I always wore a smile?
Even when I was feeling blue?

Would you tell people
I was a great friend?
Always down to rock until the bitter end?
How about you tell them,
how loyal and caring I was?
You could even throw in there my many flaws.
Despite what people could say,
doesn't change a thing.
I was sad and felt alone,
my poor stupid heart, always aching.
Just please say happy things
While my children sit and hear
All the wonderful things I was.
How I loved them so dear.
But whatever you say, don't let them know,
I had to leave and let them go.
So, hide the shot gun and the shells.
Let them think I'm going to heaven,
When I'm really going to hell.
To my kids You were
and will always be my everything.
I'm sorry... I love you...
"... the church...bells...ring" ...

My Best Friend Forever

The days go by so slowly.
I sit back and rack my brain.
Why the hell can't I shake or stop any of this pain?
The pain of being near you knowing we're just friends.
How I want to wrap my arms around you,
holding you like there's no end.
The times we've shared together,
are too far apart it seems.

But once we are together,

all the pain in my heart has seized.

You're my best friend.
Always down for me,
until the very end
I love you with all my heart.
Thanks for being there,
right from the start.
When I'm a pain in the ass
you correct me gently.

With the stern tone of your voice

Which makes me stop suddenly,
as if I had no other choice.

You keep me grounded; you keep me sane.

Time with you is always

what my heart needs.

Even though I'm a mess,

you still comfort all my pleas.
Laughing and joking with you
makes me feel safe.
Do you know I'm in love with you?

Falling of the Mask

My unconditional love
is what makes me love you.
My trauma and brokenness
are what forces me to stay.
I will never understand how you promised,
you were a different man.
You said you would never hurt me.
You promised to set my soul free.
You weren't like the other guys.
Everything that came out your mouth,
where stories and fucking lies!
I came to you my truths on the table.
You made me believe you were true.
For once I felt interpretable,
you made me feel brand new.
As time would tell,
Your truths needed to be told.
From the very beginning,
your deceit was bold.
You hid behind some image,
you forced me to believe.
I couldn't understand,
how I fell for another monster.
Was I that desperate? Was I that naive?
You fooled me, you're an imposter.
Every heartbreak, every trauma,
every fear I ever told.
A tactic used to manipulate and scare me,
Fear and control.
Never genuine love, will you ever mold.
Soon your Karma will set me free.

Unborn Child

You're my unborn child,
that I love so dear
You were a product of love,
that was shared throughout the year.
I know if I have you,
it wouldn't be fair.
You deserve a good life,
that I couldn't prepare.
Your father is gone, your mother is here.
Not only the mom,
But both parents should be near.
So unborn child,
have patience, I'll get help soon.
I'll get you out,
of your miserable cocoon.
Please don't think
I'm punishing you.
It wouldn't be pleasant
experience to go through.
But this is something that I must do.
Because I want the best life for you.
Unborn child please don't hate me,
just think, when you're gone, you'll be free.
Instead of in this hellish place,
That can't give you
what you need and want.
Even though I don't know you,
I love you and always will.
For you are my unborn child,
that I love so dear.

Misery

Leave me alone!
Your misery is not welcomed.
Being with you,
was like being a felon.
Caged without freedom,
No space for breath.
Alive in my system,
Overdose is meth
That's how dealing with you
has felt thus far.
I'm as cold as ice
ready to melt.
With vengeance and fury,
I can't be stopped.
My head is going crazy,
I'm about ready to pop.

REGRET

I should probably be angry.
I should probably be blue.
I don't regret,
Being in love with you.
I have searched with no avail,
for someone to capture my heart.
It was and has always been you.
Right from the very start.
You ask why I'm not mad,
Here is the reason why.
You never called me out my name.
You never made me cry.
You weren't like them.
You didn't treat me the same.
The situation wasn't ideal.
But when I was with you
I was able to feel.

I felt so many emotions,
all at the same time.
I'm ready to go to jail,
If loving, you were a crime.

I grow in you

I'm up right now
trying to get you out my mind.
I try to ignore "those" feelings,
But that's how we're designed.
We were destined to be lovers.
From many lifetimes ago.
I've racked my brain a million times,
that's where our love started to grow.
It's hard for me to think about
just how we fell in love.
Always there when I called for you.
You're love for me I never doubt.
I kept running away from your eyes,
that have held me captive for so long.
Always wanting and needing you
Years, and even lifetimes later,
my love for you has adapted.
I truly consider you my dearest lover and friend.
You've been beside me through it all.
My love for you is so deep it has no end.
And I continue to fucking fall.

Unfaithful Husband

I want to get over this pain,

all the lies, all the tears.

All these fucking, wasted years.

I was suffering, crying,

unable to sleep.

Some nights my kids could hear me,

just weep and weep

How could you destroy

the one person that truly loved you?

How could you pull away from me,

when you were my glue?

I tried to tell you,

my spirit would die.

I thought what we had was true.

Your face you could no longer hide.

Now, I'm so fucking done with you.

No more deceit

You were always there for me whenever I was scared.
You never made me worry,
you always showed you cared.
As time went on,
your smile soon changed.
You often came home angry, not knowing what was wrong,
I started to feel deranged.
You would yell at the kids.
Then targeted me.
So many nights of crying and fighting.
Wishing you would just let us be.
I noticed when I looked into your eyes,
I used to see my reflection.
Now all I see are lies and no more affection.
All the women, you begged to see.
All the while I'm waiting for your safe return home.
Once you stepped inside,
you would start fucking cursing at me.
All the nights I needed you,
for a warm and loving touch
You had other plans with bitches,
now you don't love me as much.
You've disrespected me,
hurt my heart, my head, my soul.
You promised to love me no matter what.
My heart you fucking stole.

Now I'm stuck trying to heal and fix me,
while you continue to fucking lie.
You haven't loved me since forever,
I thought I would surely die.
Well, as the Universe would have it,
she always knows what's best.
Your mask you could no longer hide,
and now we've come to an unrest.

The Silence

I've been trying to wrap my head around this.

Your eyes, your smile, your touch, I miss.

What happened to the love we once shared?

I thought you loved me; I thought you cared.

You have distanced yourself from me

you act like you don't want to be bothered B.

how do we go from being in love,

to barely being there?

You used to say you loved me,

even showed me too.

Ugh, I don't think there's

any getting over you

I been racking my brain, like wtf B.

I was so close to leaving my family.

I believed in you,

I thought we worked well together.

I really thought in time,

You could be my forever.

I get it, I got it, I won't make a fuss.

I just have to tell myself,

there won't ever be an us.

You where my greatest love story

You went from barely my lover to barely my homie.

Deceiver

I know I'm not the baddest,
or the cutest by far.
The love I'm still trying to give though,
is better than subpar.
You don't deserve my soul, body, or mind.
Thinking like this kind of love is hard to find.
I come to bed with a sexy dress on,
feeling a little bit cute at the most.
Your body was here,
Everything else about you was ghost.
I needed to be held or rocked softly to sleep.
You only want me when you want me,
your love I could never keep.
Instead of cuddling and loving on you
I'm up again feeling sad and blue.
I'm never going to be what you want out of life.
All you do is bring me down.
I want so bad to fix things.
You Sir are a fucking clown.
It's not my problem
for it's you that shit brings.
Yet, I suffer in pain as usual I see.
I must come to terms,
you have never truly wanted,
or ever really loved me.

The fall of the house of husband

It may seem as though I'm selfish,
It may appear as though I don't even care.
Now it's come down to my sanity,
I need a healthy life, it's only fair.
I've tried to be your friend,
your lover and your wife.
You never truly appreciated me.
Your attitude and sharpness feel like a knife.
You did things without me knowing,
it would eventually break my heart.
I thought we were in love or something.
I thought this time I was smart.
I forgave you for everything,
so many fucking times.
You not wanting to acknowledge,
Your horrible, horrible, actions
Never being held accountable for any marital crimes.
You gas lit me.
Whenever I would confront you.
All you did was lie to my face.
You were never ever truthful.
You're miserable, you're a fucking disgrace.
This "love" of yours isn't true!
Man, I'm so fucking disgusted!
I'm very much fucking done with you!

Secret Life

When do you know,
it's come to an uncertain end?
It's been some long hard years
that we've been close friends.
I started feeling more different
then I normally would.
A feeling of love
that only we understood.
I've asked myself so many times.
Why do I commit such crimes?
The crime of passion, the crime of lust.
The crime of confiding in you.
The crime of trust.
How could these be crimes you say?
The crime to think, you could be mine.
Maybe it's the feeling of anxiety.
Wanting to hear your voice
Standing, still standing...
Waiting as if I have no other choice.
The image of your eyes

The soft touch of your hand
Makes me wonder,
why you were never my man.
I often fantasized,
a whole life in my head with you.
Would we cuddle on the couch?
Would you call me your boo?
Would we watch tv, or take a walk in the park?
Would we stay up breaking night?
Laughing out loud in the dark?
Would we cook dinner together?
Set the table for two?
Would you stare in my eyes,
Saying, "Ma, I'm in love with you"?
Would we get married, living our lives
happily, and blessed?
Would we ruin our friendship
Making "us" a big mess?
Now it hit's, me sad but true
My secret lover and friend for years,
I'm deeply in love with you.

Voodoo wore off

I will love you forever.
I will think of you from time to time.
Wondering what you're doing,
and if you could see my Facebook timeline.
My heart is hurting.
I must let you go.
I'm tired of giving you love,
and feelings for me you never show.
I hope that you're happy as you live your life
also, congratulations on marrying your wife
You lied to me when there was no need
All I ever asked of you,
was no matter what, always keep it real with me.
I was stupid to think
I had you and your love was true
Until I realized you played me again for a fool
I have learned my lessons, this much is true,
You will never know how much I loved you.
You will never have a clue.
So, this is me saying farewell for now
you acted the scene perfectly,
now take your final bow.
I won't be infected, no more tears will fall from my eyes
I awaken from your voodoo; I no longer believe your lies.

Angry Wife

You know all these niggas hurt me,
broke me right down to my core.
Here you go again talking to bitches

my heart once again tore.
I'm supposed to forgive and forget,
is what you said to me.
Then you continue to hurt me,

hitting the point of no return, with no regret!
I can do all these things right back to you,
that's what you've done to me for years.
This time it's going to be you that's crying,
and no one to wipe away your miserable tears
You do nothing to be consistent
I'm always taking your little crumbs.

So, forgive me if I'm always fucking sad,
and why I'm always numb.
You were the one that was to keep me good.
Instead, you were the one who betrayed me
I tried and did all that I could.
Now leave me alone and just let me be.

Narcissist Husband

You expect me to always forgive you

When you're always breaking my heart

I can't help but remember

all the lies you told

Saying how we would never part

But every time without fail

All the love and passion

I had for you,

you managed to derail.

The times I put my trust in you,

I told you important things.

The minute you got mad at me

You would villainize and judge me

During one of your mood swings.

I've known now for years,

you never truly loved me.

Always seeing us as a burden,

before you, I had a free spirit,

my nature carefree

Your aura though,

was that of a serpent...

The Love is gone

My heart was broken for the last time.
The fact that you could even treat me unkind
not to mention extremely cruel.
My heart has always been pure and true
You no longer love me
there's nothing I can do
We go back and forth,
Of days passed and futures ahead.
I still can't shake these intrusive thoughts,
Of you making love to bitches in my bed.
I told you to treat me right,
all we ever did was fight
The more you hurt me,

the more I could see,

that this way of "loving" me,

was manipulative and mean.
After years of abuse
I found my voice
I realized I was in fact a Queen.

Twin Flame Shenanigans

It doesn't matter what time of year
Or even how long it's been,
since we last caught up with one another.
You always bring this vibe, this energy
that makes my entire body quiver.
The tip of my toes start to do this little dance
They curl up pushing a force to my legs,
ready to embrace this sweet romance.
Once my legs are weak,
I feel completely helpless.
Feelings of electricity are shooting up to my naval,
which you kiss so softly.
My hands wrap around you,
it feels like eternity.
Our souls are so happy
to feel and see,
Just what magic "we" could be.
We can't seem to keep our hands off one another
We hug, and in that moment
I'm floating on a cloud
I hold on tight, not ever wanting to let go.
When the time finally comes
To say good-bye
My heart screams out loud.

This nigga ain't shit

All alone in the darkness, all alone with strife
How in the hell could you be living,
Living a double life?
Promises you never kept
Always with other chicks
Why you always slept around?
Giving away marital dick?

Never even caring about me.
Never once wondering if we'd even live.
The two of us unhappy
The things you did to me and the kids.
The hurt, the pain, the agony.
How I thought that dying would be better.
Or being left abandoned
Shot in the head in an alley
No one to find me, no one to care
was better than the life, you couldn't prepare
Now I've found my way in life
realizing I was a wonderful wife
I smile on the surface
Because I have to,
I'm hurting inside
because you never loved me
Soon that will all go away you'll see.
All the hurt you caused, will no longer be.

A Caged Mind

My chest is tight
I can't seem to breathe
these four walls
all they do is squeeze
my head is fogging
filled with clutter,
uselessness, anger,

was once my heart a flutter.

Closing my eyes to escape the pain,
isn't really helping,
I'm still going insane.
I've been asking, begging,
finally screaming
"I need love, intimacy,
attention you fucking demon!"

How is it that you were once true?

Now I can't even stand to look at you!
My heart is broken, you could care less
what once was filled with love
is now occupied, by loneliness and sadness

Old flames never die

I know this makes zero sense
we've both racked our brains
for the millionth time.
This started when we were barely teens,

I knew then I wanted you to be mine.

Sit back and think about it though,

we always came back for each other.

Always going along with the flow
I was young minded but also,
"involved" with my child's father.

Every time I turned around

there you were to greet me.
The sneaking around,
love that was found,
we lost each other briefly.
While that time was manifesting
what would soon be our fate.
you met someone,
I had a person too
you reached out, I picked up.

We talked, laughed, and set a date.

That first time meeting

After years was my biggest fear.
You embraced me with that,
"old school love"

You know TRUE love that never disappears?

The one that fairy tales are made of

think about it Louie, we're destined to be.

We've been through mad shit

I know you're truly in love with me.

Anxiety in my head

There's this feeling of uncertainty that lurks,
creeps and hides inside of me. '
I feel like I'm alone
on a journey that's not too kind
I want to never look back, just leave abruptly.
I'm certain if I did leave, nobody would even mind.
I drift someplace quiet, loving, and pleasant.
Where everyone is smiling and kind.
A place with tall trees, statues and pretty faces
instead of this place that's dark and miserable
just weird open spaces
I didn't ask to be here
yet Here I am alone
I just want to disappear
like a cold winter nights storm
No one notices my vanishing act,
I left behind a clone
instead of suffering alone,
no one to hear me moan
I'm walking in this dark,
In what appears to be a hallway
I can vaguely hear a whisper
I finally make out
that it's telling me not to stay then…I hear a faint whimper…

Point of no return

Remember this smile,
when I'm no longer here
My laughter, my life,
will no longer flow through your ear.
Remember these eyes
the secrets they hold,
for the love,
you didn't care to mold
I was forced to hide, the secrets you keep
Remember my tears?

How I would weep and weep.
Remember my spirit? Lively and free
I will never understand
why you did this to me.
As I sit here exhausted, tired, and hurt
this once free spirit, turned introvert
is about to end your reign of abuse
Ima take this raging bull and put it to good use…

His eyes never lie

Something is bothering me
What do I do?
How the fuck,
could I even fall for you?
I don't really know who you are.
We've never discussed us this far
How are we both in love?
How could this be?
I can't be with you,
I'm married
We would lay in bed together
Me wanting this to last forever
Something in your eyes
Something that never lies
But your actions they hurt
What was this? Just a flirt?
When our bodies would meet
It was hard to be discreet
I just wanted your body to touch mine
How you kissed me, Oh, so fine.
Knowing nothing about each other life
How could it be, I wanted to be your wife
Confused about you, knowing how I felt
We had a crazy hand
the Universe dealt
Time passes thinking of you
From time to time
Wondering why, I didn't make you mine
I know eventually
You would cause me pain
Being with you would make me insane

We Belong together

We're bonded for real for real
Why can't you see?
That when we're not together
You're thinking of me?
As I distract you, my mind is full
Of days and love, I've spent with you
Then when we finally get a chance to reunite
Our souls transcend and take flight!
The question is how many more years,
How many situations do we have to go through?
For you to see
I belong to you, and you belong to me?

A Family Affair

As I turn the pages on pictures from long ago
I can't help but look into the eyes of those
Around me
If you look close enough, really, deep enough
Their eyes, tell a story
Looking back on childhood memories
Family was all around
Block parties, outings to the park,
All the major holidays
Remembering in real time
how I wanted to be loved like this always
The feeling of security, love and family
Not knowing that there was a storm brewing
Slowly creeping, eventually manifesting
Into a demon the size of New York City
The family I once held near, held dear to my heart
Was violently, aggressively being torn apart
No goodbyes, no hugs, no see you later gator
No warm smiles, no more familiar faces
No more fun exciting places
These pictures, they hold a secret indeed
While yes, we smiled it looked so effortlessly
But deeper behind their eyes
Nobody really cared, loved,
Or even fucked with me
I'm a product of two selfish people
Who pretended to care
Who looked me in my eyes
Ands said they would ALWAYS be there…

"Eventually my heart would be so wounded, from negligence and abandonment. I had thoughts of a different   time and place; I felt my love was inadequate. Upon digging deep, and deeper still, I couldn't even remember, just how I fell for you. Now, I'm beginning to think, my whole life was just a fucking lie. How do you ask? It's easy, I have a story to tell. How I was "married" to this Narcissist. But the whole time I was in love with another guy."

Made in United States
North Haven, CT
13 September 2024

57363463R00029